SUMMER CAMP

Summer Camp is published by Stone Arch Books,
A Capstone Imprint
1710 Roe Crest Drive
North Mankato, Minnesota 56003

Library of Congress Cataloging-in-Publication Data

Names: Brandes, Wendy L., 1965- author. | Lorenzet, Eleonora, illustrator.
Title: MJ's camp crisis / by Wendy L. Brandes
Description: North Mankato, Minnesota : Stone Arch Books, an imprint of Capstone Press, [2017] | Series: Summer camp | Summary: When twelve-year-old MJ signed up for seven weeks at Camp Mon Mon Lake, she thought her best friend was going too, but now she feels like an extra whee—things get a little better when another new girl, Zoe, arrives, butthen MJ reveals the secret that Zoe is anxious to hide, and MJ suddenly feels very isolated and lonely.
Identifiers: LCCN 2016020952| ISBN 9781496525987 (library binding) | ISBN 9781496527110 (pbk.) | ISBN 9781496527158 (ebook (pdf))
Subjects: LCSH: Camps—Juvenile fiction. | Secrecy—Juvenile fiction. Social isolation—Juvenile fiction. | Loneliness—Juvenile fiction. |Friendship—Juvenile fiction. | CYAC: Camps—Fiction. | Secrets—Fiction.| Loneliness—Fiction. | Friendship—Fiction.
Classification: LCC PZ7.1.B7515 Mj 2017 | DDC 813.6 [Fic] —dc23v
LC record available at https://lccn.loc.gov/2016020952

Illustrated by Eleonora Lorenzet

Printed and bound in the USA
009661CGF16

SUMMER CAMP

MJ'S CAMP CRISIS

BY WENDY L. BRANDES

STONE ARCH BOOKS
a capstone imprint

FIND YOUR ADVENTURE AT

CAMP MON MON LAKE!

Camp Mon Mon Lake, an all-girls sleepaway camp in Maine, has it all! Girls return year after year for friendship, challenges, and fun. And every year, they take home memories of a magical summer filled with the warmth of a summer family.

We group our campers according to age. Each group is assigned a different bird name—and there are A LOT of different birds up here! Our youngest group is the Hummingbirds (ages 7–8) and our oldest group is the Condors, also known as the Seniors (ages 14–15). In between we have Blue Jays, Robins, and Songbirds.

At Mon Mon Lake, we fill the weeks with singing, spirit, activity, and group bonding. No matter what your interests are, we have an activity for you!

MON MON'S SUMMER ACTIVITIES

LAND SPORTS

ARCHERY
BASKETBALL
CLIMBING WALL
FIELD HOCKEY
GYMNASTICS
LACROSSE
RIDING
SOCCER
SOFTBALL
TENNIS
VOLLEYBALL
YOGA

WATER SPORTS

CANOEING
KAYAKING
SAILING
SWIMMING
WATERSKIING

THE ARTS

DANCE
DRAMA
DRAWING
PAINTING
POTTERY

WHAT CAMPERS ARE SAYING:

"I didn't want to come to camp at all, but that's before I met my bunkmates. The girls at Camp Mon Mon make the best friends."
— MJ, a new camper

I love the swimming, the intercamp games, and all the fun in the bunk—especially pranking our counselors!"
— Emily, a four-year camp veteran

"I love the group shows. Being onstage in front of the entire camp—and the boys' camp next door—is amazing! No place is more fun than Camp Mon Mon Lake!"
— Nina, a Blue Jay (age 13)

"The camp trips are my favorite part about camp. What could be better than hiking and camping out with your best friends?"
— Claire, award winner for Best Outdoorswoman

CHAPTER 1

This was not turning out like it was supposed to. No way would I have signed up for seven weeks at Camp Mon Mon Lake if I knew that my best friend Ariel was going to bail at the last second. Yeah, a family trip to China is hard to pass up, but still.

So here I was, riding solo on a bus to a camp I've never seen—with way too many overly enthusiastic girls! Why did I let Ari convince me to go?

I liked to spend my summers lounging around. Hanging with my older brother Eli, getting annoyed by my younger sister Isabelle, going to Yankees games, traveling upstate to see my Aunt Martha and swim in her

pool. Maybe a day camp or two. I know that no one would think it was very exciting, but it worked fine for me.

And I wanted this summer to be like the last few. Especially after this school year, when everybody seemed to be different. This year, boys who were my good friends suddenly forgot that I existed. Another one of my best friends, Rebecca, decided that Ariel and I weren't cool and ditched us for the popular kids. Unpopular kids suddenly became popular, and vice versa. Did I want to deal with a bunch of new people this summer? Definitely not. But here I was, alone on a bus, thanks to Ariel's unexpected family trip.

I was about to put in my earbuds and try to zone out to Stained Glass Collision's new album when an older-looking girl plopped herself down next to me. "Hi there! I'm Bick. You're new, right? Are you in the Blue Jays?"

I made a snap decision and said, "I'm MJ." I wasn't sure where the name came from. No one has ever called

BUS STOP
01

me MJ. But if I was going to keep up with someone named Bick, I had to start somewhere. And MJ sounded way cooler than Madeline Jenkins.

"How old are you?" Bick asked.

"Twelve," I answered. "You?"

"Turning fourteen next week," she said. "I'm a Songbird this year."

I nodded, trying to remember the different names for each age group.

"You got on the bus in New York City, right? Are you from there or did you come in from Long Island or New Jersey?" Bick asked.

"From the burbs," I said. "You?"

"N-Y-C," she said, exaggerating her accent. "I've been going to Mon Mon for three years."

"Mon Mon?" I asked.

"Yeah, our camp! Camp Mon Mon Lake!" Bick laughed. "Don't worry newbie, we'll show you the ropes! You know about first night snake line and the Condors' senior theme, right?"

I shook my head. "All I know is there's a lake," I said. "But I can't wait to see it all!" Fake enthusiasm. Maybe that's the way to deal with all of these super-über camper types.

"You'll love it!" She began listing activities. "The camp shows, the singing, color war, the hiking trip—so much fun stuff! Plus, you might get a camp sister."

"Like someone older who'll show me around and help me adjust?"

"No, silly, you'd be the older sister."

I swallowed hard. How could I be a camp sister when I was so new?

"Great!" I said, faking it again. Only 48 and a half days left.

Five hours and fifty camp songs later, we got off the bus. The second my feet touched the gravel road, I was buried in a sea of older girls. They were singing a song that had words like *pep, best, sisters, summer,* and, of course, *Camp Mon Mon Lake*. To make things worse, they were jumping up and down and giving random hugs. I am definitely *not* a random hugger.

When the singing ended, one of the counselors took me and a few of the other new girls to the Main House. The owner of the camp, who everyone called Aunt Alice, was waiting to greet us. Aunt Alice was between my mom and my grandma's age and had this crazy, curly, gray hair, which was peeking out from a fishing cap.

When we walked in, she jumped out of her chair and gave us a big Camp Mon Mon Lake welcome. "MMM-LO, MMM-LO. A big MMMMM hello!" I didn't understand half of what she said after that—it sounded like some sort of weird bibbity-bobbity language. I was *never* going to get used to all the singing and strange talking.

Next, Aunt Alice went down the line of new campers and said something to each of us. When she got to me, she whispered, "I know you expected your friend to be here, and this must all seem very strange to you, dear. But I promise, in no time you'll be a part of all of it." She gave me a big hug and then walked me over to meet my group leader, who introduced herself as Rachel Richardson.

Rachel—whom I immediately thought of as R^2 with her double-R initials—spoke really fast in a singsong voice. Basically in one breath, she said, "I went here, you know, for nine years. I started way younger than you. And now, I'm back. Do you like theater by the way? I wanna be a set designer. Oh, and I'm a junior in college. And I love Harry Potter. Now you. Tell me everything I need to know about you, Madeline."

"You can call me MJ," I said. "And I've never described myself as quickly as you just did."

She laughed. Maybe I could be the funny kid?

"Hit the highlights, then," R^2 said.

"I'm a baseball fanatic. Love dogs. I have an older brother and a younger sister." I felt my throat close a little when I mentioned Eli and Isabelle. Crud. I definitely did not want to be the kid who cried. Especially on the first day. Totally babyish.

R^2 must have sensed the sniffling, because she started blah-blah-blahing about camp even faster as she led me to my bunk. To keep the waterworks away, I tried to focus on what she was saying. What I heard was "Bunk 12a," "Four other girls," "Two counselors."

By the time we had finished walking down the hill to my bunk, I felt a little less like I had to cry.

"Here it is, your Blue Jay home for the summer!" R^2 threw her arms open in a big gesture.

When R^2 opened the door to the bunk, holiday bells tinkled. "Oh, those are there because your bunk has a sleepwalker," R^2 said. As soon as that was out of her mouth, she tried to take it back. "Whoops. I'm pretty sure I wasn't supposed to tell you that."

"I'll keep it quiet," I promised. "But why exactly do we need bells for a sleepwalker?"

"If she wanders out of the bunk at night, the counselors will know that she left," R^2 explained.

"Is that really a thing? Sleepwalking?" I asked. "I thought that was something they put in movies or books to make the plot move along."

Rachel laughed. “It really is a thing. Anyway, there’s one other camper in your bunk who’s new. Her name is Zoe. She’s from London.”

There were five beds for campers and a bunk bed for the counselors. I looked around for my blue batik comforter and found it on a bed near the back of the bunk. Someone had unpacked the trunk that we sent up to camp last week. I noticed my other stuff up on shelves above the bed. A piece of yellow construction paper with my name on it was taped to the wall. I was going to have to switch that from *Madeline* to *MJ*.

“Sometime before dinner, you have to change into your camp uniform,” R^2 said. “Blue shorts and a gray top or the other way around.”

I know some of the more fashion-obsessed girls would hate that, but I didn’t mind. I’m mostly a T-shirt and jeans kind of gal. “I’m perfectly happy to be as dorky as everyone else,” I said. R^2 laughed.

MADELINE
ZOE

As I started pulling stuff out of my carry-on bag, there was a tinkle of bells and a bang of a door opening. Then two girls ran in and tackled me.

CHAPTER 3

"This is going to be the best summer!" one of the girls shouted. The other girl was doing the bibbity-bobbity greeting cheer.

Great. More hugging. And more cheering.

"I'm MJ," I said.

The bibbity-bobbity girl said, "My name is Nina and that's Claire. We're your bunkmates!"

"Rachel Richardson!" Claire singsonged. "We're stealing MJ, okay?" They started pulling me outside.

"I was just, you know, putting my stuff down. Maybe I should stay and unpack my bag," I said.

But neither girl let go. Clearly, I didn't have any choice but to go with them.

"You can do that later!" Claire said.

"We'll show you around and introduce you to people," Nina said. "Have you met anyone yet?" she asked as we walked toward the middle of camp.

I shook my head. "Just girls from the bus."

"We have a great bunk. Well, at least *we* think it's going to be a great bunk. There's the two of us, of course," Nina started.

"And we're clearly great," Claire said. She threw her arm around Nina. "Then there's Emily. She's got a big personality and loves pranks, but she's super-sweet once you get to know her."

Big personality and pranks? That sounded like it could add up to mean girl, not super-sweet.

"Don't forget her super-cute brother," Nina added.

"Her brother is capital H-O-T hot," Claire said. "But don't ever say that in front of Emily. It drives her crazy."

"Have you met him?" I asked.

Nina nodded. "He goes to Camp Eagle Rock across the lake. You know, our brother camp? The one we have socials with?"

"Socials? You mean dances?" I asked. "Totally weird and awkward, right?"

"Awkward, for sure!" Claire said. "Neens, remember when Ashley was dancing with Nate last year and—"

"Yes!" Nina, replied cracking up. "That was so hilarious!"

"What happened?" I asked, totally lost.

"Oh, it was no biggie. Too hard to explain," Nina said.

"Okay," I said, feeling two steps behind.

"Anyway, we're here!" Claire made a sweeping gesture with her arm. Dead ahead was a gorgeous lake. A line of boats sat waiting to be taken out on the sparkling water.

"Wow! This is amazing!" I said. It really was. No act at all. Totally beautiful and like nothing I'd ever seen. "Do you guys sail? Or canoe?" I hadn't thought of doing

either of those things until just this moment, but seeing the boats definitely made me feel better.

Maybe this camp stuff wasn't going to be so bad. Sure, these two were a little too enthusiastic and had too many inside jokes, but they might be fun. And the lake could be a blast—and maybe an escape if needed.

"I really don't like to swim," Nina said, interrupting my thoughts. "I hate how the fish come right below you. And sometimes they even brush against your leg. Plus, the water smells."

"Don't listen to her. The fish don't bother you, and the lake is the best on a really hot day. It doesn't smell. Well, not that much, anyway," Claire added.

Some other girls down at the beach waved to Claire and Nina, who waved back. Before I could ask who they were, a black lab trotted up to us. He stopped in front of me and dumped an incredibly smelly, incredibly dead fish right on my feet.

Nina freaked out and ran. Claire just stood there cracking up. And I just stared at the dead thing lying on my shoes. It was like I was paralyzed. Plus, the smell made me want to puke.

"That's Zeus. He's like the camp mascot," Claire explained once she caught her breath. "He belongs to Aunt Alice's son." Claire gave the wet dog a pat, then smelled her hand and wrinkled her nose. The dog picked up the fish and headed down the beach.

The fish smell seemed to have attached itself to my sneakers. It smelled so bad, and I wasn't sure how I was going to get it out. Was I going to be Dead Fish Girl for the rest of the summer?

"Could he get sick from the fish?" I asked, as we caught up to Nina, who was waiting a short distance away.

"Probably. But he's used to it. He's a major garbage eater. I've definitely seen him hurl a few times every summer," Claire replied.

"Let's go before he comes back and shakes smelly water all over us," Nina begged. We took a few steps and Nina said, "Something smells awful."

I knew it was me—Dead Fish Girl and my fishy sneakers. But I acted like I had no idea what she was talking about.

"Have you been coming here since you were Hummingbirds?" I asked, changing the subject.

Nina nodded. "Yes, both of us. There are ten of us lifers out of the twenty in our group. Everybody is great."

"Well, almost everybody," Claire added.

"True, there's Mac," Nina said. "But she's not so bad."

"Not so bad? She narced on us last year for trying to get in the kitchen after hours. We were only going to get some of those amazing cookies," Claire said. "Plus she was so messy. Never willing to clean up her stuff."

Uh-oh. I was certainly not the neatest. "You're all not super-clean or anything?"

"Well, *she* is," Nina said, pointing at Claire.

"I just like my own stuff to be neat," Claire protested.

"Yeah—yours and everyone else's!" Nina exclaimed.

When we arrived back at the bunk, a tall girl darted up from one of the beds. "You're Madeline, right?" she said. "You don't look like a Zoe!" Before I could say anything, she wrinkled her nose. "Who got too close to a dead fish?"

I looked around to see if there was anything I could pin it on. Nope.

"It was me. I'm MJ," I said. "Are you Emily?"

"The one and only!" She was about three inches taller than me, super-athletic looking and very, very blond. "We're excited to have you in the bunk even if you do smell like the inside of an aquarium!"

"I don't always smell this way," I said weakly. Just 48 and a quarter days to go.

By dinnertime everyone had arrived except for our mystery bunkmate, Zoe from London. So far everyone seemed nice enough, but I definitely felt like the Dead Fish Girl who didn't quite belong (even though I had changed my shoes). All of the singing was still weirding me out. And hanging with the three girls from my bunk who were already total besties was giving me a bit of a stomachache.

Still, I was trying to give everyone the benefit of the doubt and not start snap judging. I had dealt with way too much of that this year in school. I kept saying to myself, "Stay open minded."

Our bunk went to the dining hall as a group and sat at the table reserved for bunk 12a. The dining hall was cute with cool lanterns hanging from the ceiling and pictures of birds covering the walls. But it was packed way too full of wooden chairs and ugly yellow tables. Looking around, I crossed my fingers that the food wouldn't be too gross.

We sat down and the singing began immediately.

More songs? Is there a song for everything? I wondered.

Our whole table got up to sing the Blue Jay theme song. I just stood there and clapped and tried to figure out some of the words. I was able to make out *spirit, blue jay, dawn,* and something that sounded like *exhaust pipe*. I was never going to learn these correctly. I'd probably be singing about car mufflers while everyone else was singing about being friends forever.

At what seemed to be the end of the song, everyone sat down. I did too. Then they all got up again and sang the last little bit. I stayed in my chair, feeling like I just didn't get it.

"Don't worry, MJ," Nina whispered. "You'll get into it."

I nodded as if I believed her.

The songs seemed endless. For Aunt Alice there was a sweet song: "Past days of summer have faded away, but our memories of Alice remain." For the head of the waterfront, Angus, there was a rowdy song: "Angus Beef, Angus Cattle, From Sydney, Australia, you do battle." R^2 had some elaborate song about dragons and wizards or something. I could barely catch two words of that one. Who had time to write these things?

In the middle of spaghetti and meatballs, the new girl from London, Zoe, arrived. She hadn't changed into her camp uniform yet and was wearing a loose-fitting, flowing brown shirt that looked kind of designer-ish. I wondered for a second if she had come all the way here by herself or if she had just said goodbye to her parents a few minutes ago. She slipped into the chair next to me during the Robins' group song and whispered, "I'm Zoe. Are we allowed to talk while they're singing?"

"I have absolutely no idea! I'm MJ—the other newbie." She stuck out her hand like I was supposed to shake it. Maybe that was how they did stuff in London. I was disappointed that she didn't speak with an accent. I was expecting, "Where's the loo," and, "Cheerio."

Strangely, I had this weird feeling that I had met her before. Maybe in preschool or something? Maybe she just looked a bit like someone from home.

"Wait till you hear the singy hello greeting and all of the songs for different people. It's like a different planet," I said.

She laughed. "I know. That hello rhyme keeps going through my head."

Just as she said that, the table next to us erupted with a song about a pig. "Look!" she said, pointing. Someone (was that Bick from the bus!?) crawled under the table, while the rest of the girls sang, "Under the table you must go!"

Zoe looked at me and we both giggled. "Do you think we'll end up being like them?"

"Only if you crawl under the table first!" I said.

Although some of the lifers were starting to look at us, we cracked up again. Total bonding moment!

After dinner we went to the social hall. The Condors—the oldest group—revealed their theme for the summer: movie stars. Nina explained that the Condors would have activities based on the theme and, of course, create songs. Let me guess: that would lead to more singing.

Zoe sat on one side of me with Nina on the other. Nina was taking the Condors' presentation super seriously, while Zoe kept nudging me when something out of the ordinary happened (like when Alanis, the arts and crafts counselor, walked on stage wearing a bear mask and Jessica, the head counselor, juggled grapefruits). I was glad someone besides me thought this was all a little weird.

Finally, after the Condors sang their senior song, Emily came charging at us. "There you are!" Emily said. "We're about to make a snake line around the entire camp and sing 'Friends, Friends, Friends.'"

"Okay," I said slowly. "Real snakes are not involved, right?" Who knew with this place? They seemed to have all these weird traditions.

"You'll see," Claire said. "Come on."

The Condors got everyone up and asked all the campers to find their bunkmates. We all joined hands to make a line. The giant chain started with the youngest group, the Hummingbirds. Because the Blue Jays were older, we were one of the last groups to leave the social hall. We roped our way through the camp, singing a

song I actually knew. "Friends, friends, friends, we will always be . . ."

I looked at my bunkmates: Claire, Emily, Zoe, and Nina. I hoped we would all like each other enough to *become* friends. But at this point, I wasn't even sure if I was going to make it past day 47.

CHAPTER 5

After the snake line, we went back to the bunk. Susannah and Astrid, our counselors, pulled us all together into the center of the small room. We sat in a circle, and Astrid passed around a package of cookies.

Once everyone had a cookie, Susannah said, "We're going to talk rules now."

"The way to make sure our bunk stays happy at camp is to make some bunk rules," Astrid said.

"First up," Susannah jumped back in, "we need to discuss chores. We created a chore wheel for all of you. We have inspections every day. The neatest cabin each week is awarded honors. If one of you forgets to do your

job, it's up to the others to pick up the slack. Now let's move on to the rest of the rules."

Susannah seemed like she was in the army. We were really going to do someone else's chores if they didn't feel like it? Seemed crazy to me.

"Well," Emily volunteered, "we've always had the rule here that private stuff is private. Don't go through anyone's letters or emails or stuff like that."

We all nodded. I definitely didn't want anyone looking at letters I wrote home. Especially if I was unhappy. On a big piece of paper, Astrid wrote, *Respect privacy.*

"Wait a second. We get emails?" Zoe asked.

"Parents and friends can send them to us, but we can't email them back. The camp office gets the emails, prints them out, and the Sparrows sort and deliver them," Nina said.

"You know how things are around here. No Internet. No electricity. No technology. No nothing," Claire added.

"What other rules do we want?" Astrid asked. She sent the cookies around again.

"No sharing toothbrushes or hairbrushes. Remember we had that whole lice thing last year," Emily said with a little shiver.

"*Ew.* Yes, yes, yes. Absolutely no sharing brushes!" Nina exclaimed, shuddering.

Lice? Really? Lice? I had a sudden case of the heebie-jeebies. How was I going to get through this whole camp thing when lice was *actually* a possibility?

Then Claire raised her hand. "This is kind of awkward, but as the only black person in this bunk I have to say it. If anyone mentions Martin Luther King, Jr. or Barack Obama or Oprah or any other famous black person, please do not turn to look at me. I hate that." She smiled. "That's all."

It took me a second to realize that I hadn't seen too much diversity at the camp. And, wow, I've never heard someone be so straightforward about race like that! It was pretty awesome.

Susannah wrote, *Be sensitive to others' culture and heritage.*

"What about pranks?" Emily asked after a minute.

"What about them?" Susannah said.

"Are they okay? Will people get mad if I play a prank on them?"

That made me a little nervous. With an older brother, I've gotten pranked, of course. Sometimes Eli's pranks were mean, though.

Zoe must have been anxious too. "What do you mean by pranks?" she asked. "Are you thinking of switching our soap so it turns our skin blue or putting shaving cream on our pillows? Because I don't think I'd like that."

Emily grinned. "Well, I have done pranks like that, but maybe we could say no pranks that might affect someone's personal appearance."

"What about no pranking your bunkmates at all," Nina said, crossing her arms.

"Aw, c'mon, that's no fun," Emily pouted.

"What about no pranks for the first week," I said. "You know, let us newbies get used to camp before you start messing with our minds." I didn't want to sound like a bad sport, but I also didn't want to wake up with my bed in the middle of camp or possibly in the middle of the lake!

Emily grinned again. "Don't you and Zoe want to go through Mon Mon initiation?"

"Quit making them nervous, Emily. There's no such thing as Mon Mon initiation," Nina said.

Still grinning, Emily said, "I'm just playing. You don't have to worry about me. No pranks." She stopped and then added, "For a week."

"Thanks," I said. I raised my eyebrows as if to say, "I'll be watching you."

RULE

We talked some more about rules and then started to get ready for bed. The cabins at Mon Mon were really basic. We had a bathroom with two sinks and two toilets, which wasn't too bad until everyone was trying to get ready for bed at once. Then things got crowded! Even though Eli, Isabelle and I fought over bathroom time, it was nothing compared to this.

No electricity meant that we had light only until the sun went down. Then it was time to get out the flashlights. I wasn't sure how it was going to work to brush my teeth while holding a flashlight. But Susannah had a headlamp that she let us all use. We looked pretty dorky, but at least our teeth were clean.

Once I was all ready for bed, I started worrying about what it would be like to sleep with so many people in one room. Would I even be able to sleep? I got under my covers, carefully examining my sheets for insects and other crawly things.

Ten minutes later Astrid and Susannah said goodnight. "Flashlights off in fifteen!" Astrid said as they left the cabin.

"Where are you going? Don't you sleep here?" Zoe asked while they were still within earshot.

"Once you're asleep, we *do* get some time off, you know," Susannah said. She said it like she was stuck with us. Susannah was definitely slightly annoying.

"One of us is OD—on duty—to cover the bunk," Astrid explained. "If we are OD, we sit on the porch or walk around the camp and look in on different bunks. So don't think you can stay up as late as you want!" she said, grinning.

They left and the door tinkled behind them, which made me wonder again who the sleepwalker was. We all played flashlight tag on the ceiling for a bit when Emily noticed that Nina's light hadn't moved for a while. Emily shined her flashlight on Nina's sleeping face, just when Nina was making a weird little snort. We all laughed.

"Sometimes there's snoring, but we just let it slide," Emily said.

What if *I* snored? Would they let the newbie slide? I turned off my flashlight and counted backward from 47.

At seven the next morning, five of the Condors let themselves into our bunk. "Wake up! Wake up! It's time for the scavenger hunt!" They dropped sunglasses with blue or gray tips on everyone's beds before dashing out. Zoe and I had blue sunglasses.

"What's this all about?" Zoe asked.

Emily poked her head out of the bathroom and said, "Scavenger hunt!" before disappearing again.

"Got that part," Zoe said, rolling her eyes.

"There are two teams," Claire explained. "It looks like Emily, Nina, and I are on the Gray team. You're on Blue. You look for stuff around camp with your teammates.

The team that gets the most stuff on its list before time runs out wins the hunt."

"It's the most fun ever!" Nina added.

"Wear your blue clothes—shirts *and* shorts!" Emily called from the bathroom. "Hurry!"

Within fifteen minutes of finishing breakfast, the Blue team was meeting out on the main lawn. We had a list of more than three hundred things that we were supposed to find. The Condors divided the list and assigned partners. I was partnered with Zoe and Bick, the girl I had met on the bus.

Our list had crazy stuff on it. *Poo-poo paper. A four-leaf clover. A macramé bracelet. An ice skate* (at a summer camp?). *A signed picture of Derek Jeter.*

"What's poo-poo paper?" I asked.

"Art paper made from elephant poop," Bick said.

We cracked up. "How do you know this, and who here has it?" Zoe asked.

Bick was all business. “Angus has poo-poo paper. He likes to use it for his sketches. Zoe, run and find Angus and get some of his paper.”

“On it!” Zoe saluted. “Well . . . I would be, but I don’t know who Angus is.”

“Newbies! He’s the giant six-and-a-half-foot-tall waterfront counselor. And he is totally hot,” Bick said.

“Super-tall, super-hot. Got it. And where do I find him?”

“Just go! He’s tall! You’ll see his head over the tree tops!” Bick shooed Zoe away. “Go, go, go!”

Zoe ran off. “Next,” Bick said. “Where do we find Derek Jeter or an ice skate?”

“I actually may have a Derek Jeter baseball card,” I offered. “It might have a preprinted autograph. Would that count?”

“Yes! Go!" she shouted. "Meet back here!”

I ran to my empty bunk. I grabbed my folder full of stamps, pencils, and stationery and dumped it out on my bed. Derek had to be in here somewhere. I found a whole bunch of other stuff. Other baseball cards, school pictures, photos of my family, a dried flower from our trip to Hawaii, and clippings of my favorite bands.

As my eyes passed over a photo of Stained Glass Collision posing in a deserted subway, it hit me—the reason why I thought Zoe was familiar. Zoe was Chase Wagner's daughter! Chase Wagner, lead singer for Stained Glass Collision, probably one of the most famous guys on the planet! I was sharing a bunk with the kid of a super-celeb!

Ariel was going to flip if she ever came to camp. And Eli—I'd have to tell Eli. Would Chase come on visiting day? Could I get him to sign my band T-shirt? Would he be here, in this bunk?

I took a deep breath. *Focus*, I thought. *No more thinking about Zoe's famous dad until the scavenger hunt is done!*

I found my Derek Jeter card, complete with a printed signature on the front. Hopefully it would be good enough. I ran out the door and sprinted to find Bick. She was by the flagpole where I left her, on her hands and knees looking for a four-leaf clover.

I stretched out my hand with the card as I doubled over gasping for breath.

She grabbed it and squealed. "This is perfect! You're so amazing. Let's hope Zoe gets here soon! Now on to the ice skate!"

"Where," I paused, still catching my breath, "do you think we could find that?"

"I know Tammy Ellis in the Sparrows skates competitively in the winter. But I'm pretty sure that she's on Gray anyway, and I can't think why she'd bring skates to camp."

"What about a skate on a keychain? Would that count?" I asked.

"Do you know where we can get one? I think—" Bick was interrupted by Zoe, as out of breath as I had been. She held out a pad of paper. I was disappointed that it looked like regular paper. I gave it a sniff, but it just smelled like paper.

"Yay!" Bick and I both cheered. Zoe started laughing through her gasps.

Bick happily snatched the paper out of Zoe's hand and did a little victory twirl. "I got the two best newbies at camp! Two items done. D-O-N-E!"

"Should we start looking for the four-leaf clover? That's going to be hard. H-A-R-D!" I said, imitating Bick.

"No, first we get the macramé bracelet," Bick said.

"I noticed some boy counselor wearing one last night," Zoe said.

"Which one?" Bick asked.

Zoe shrugged. "Tall, really skinny. I think his sister is a camper."

"Think! Where'd you see him? Waterfront? Land sports? Tennis?" Bick asked.

"Tennis, I think?" Zoe didn't sound so sure, but with Bick, hesitation was not an option.

"Then run girls!" Bick commanded. "Look for Mr. No-Name on the tennis court."

"What if it's a friendship bracelet or something he can't take off?" I asked.

"Promise him you'll make him a new one. Or cut his whole arm off. Now go!"

"Yes, General!" I saluted, and Zoe laughed.

We jogged over to the tennis courts. No luck. The courts were empty.

"Any ideas?" I asked Zoe.

"We cannot let General Bick and the mighty Blue team down!" Zoe said. "Plus, did you hear what she said about the friendship bracelet? She might cut our arms off too if we don't find it!"

We both laughed now. I realized that I was actually having fun.

"Maybe we could make one," I suggested.

"Do you know where the Arts and Crafts building is?" she asked.

"No clue!"

"I don't either!" she exclaimed.

"We're terrible at this!" I laughed as we high-fived.

I couldn't believe how easy it was to hang out with Zoe. But it was too weird—the idea of getting closer to her, knowing who she was. I probably already knew her answers to lots of questions you'd normally ask someone. Not that I was her dad's stalker or anything, but at home, I do have downtime and a computer. Like, I already knew she had a cockapoo named Rex and a cat named Patches.

Couldn't she just go back to being regular Zoe? My new friend who I really liked. I mean, I wouldn't want anyone to judge me because of my parents. I almost laughed out loud at the idea of someone Googling my mom or dad. Weird.

"I have an idea," she said, interrupting my thoughts. "I have a lanyard that I think is macramé or macramé-ish. It has a hook on the end for keys, but I think we could make it look like a bracelet somehow. Do you think it would count?"

"Show me."

We ran down the hill to the bunk and went straight to Zoe's dresser. She rifled through her stuff and pulled open a plastic box.

"My locket with my dog's hair! Look!" she cried.

"Dog's hair? For real?" I said.

"I thought it was funny," she replied.

"Concentrate, Zoe! Keep looking!"

"Here! Look at this!" she exclaimed.

"You found it?"

"No, but look at my lucky shell! It's shaped like a heart!"

"Focus, Zoe!" I said. "Remember, we are looking for your macramé-ish bracelet thing!"

"Right, right!" She sorted through more stuff, while I wondered whether her dad had picked out some of these things for her.

Finally, she dumped everything onto her bed and held up the lanyard. "What do you think?"

"Let's try."

We ran out and found Bick.

Bick looked at it and frowned. "We'll use this as a last resort. If you bump into the boy counselor, grab him. Otherwise, we have to move on to four-leaf clovers. Go to the soccer field. It's right next to tennis. That's the best place to start."

We ran to the field, plopped down about five feet from each other and started looking.

"Have you ever done this before? Scavengering?" Zoe asked me.

"Once, at my school a few years ago. And guess what happened? We had our team's pile of stuff on a blanket on the football field and a squirrel came and grabbed one of the rice crackers we found!"

"That's hilarious!"

"I know, right?! I'm not a big fan of squirrels, for sure. But I love most other animals," I said.

"Do you have any pets?" she asked.

"We have a pug named Kreider. You?" I knew she'd tell me about Patches and Rex, but it would've been rude not to ask.

Should I just tell her that I know who her dad is? I wondered. No, it might make things awkward between us. I already felt awkward enough just being at Mon Mon.

As we were looking, Emily and Claire came running up. Gray teamers!

"What are you guys hunting for?" Emily asked.

"Four-leaf clover. You guys?" I asked.

"First place trophy for any land sport against Camp Wildfoot," Claire said. "We're going to try the Don."

"Should we know what that means?" Zoe asked.

Thank goodness I wasn't the only one who didn't understand half of what the lifers were saying. So glad that Zoe was with me.

Claire laughed. "Sorry, sometimes I forget that we speak another language here. The Don is the 'Donald G. Murphy Recreational Center.' Everyone calls it the Don."

"You guys having fun?" Emily asked.

"Working hard!" Zoe replied and I giggled.

"We're outta here! C'mon Claire," Emily said, pulling Claire's arm. "We gotta go. 'Beat the Blue, Beat the Blue, Gray will always come through!'" They both waved and yelled goodbye as they ran off.

"Should I be scared of Emily?" Zoe asked.

I laughed. "She definitely has a competitive spirit, but yesterday Claire and Nina told me how great she is."

"I have a friend like her in London. Kind of bossy sometimes, but mostly a mushball the rest of the time."

"That's funny, because the bossy girls at my school are just plain bossy!" I said.

Zoe laughed. "We have those too. I stay away from them. But the mean girls don't bother with me."

"Because?" I asked. Maybe she'd just say it. *Because you're Chase Wagner's daughter.*

"Because I don't react to them." She shrugged and went back to peering into the clover.

I wondered if that was true. Or if she believed it was true. It must be weird not to know if people treat you differently because your dad is famous.

We kept talking. Maybe our bonding spurred both of us to look harder, because about ten minutes later, I found it! A four-leaf clover! We jumped up and down, but

carefully, because we didn't want any of the leaves to fall off our treasure!

"I wish I had a cell so I could take a selfie of us with our little piece of good luck!" Zoe yelled.

We ran-walked back to Bick. She screamed and did some Blue team cheer: "Blue team, blue team, CMML's best. We'll bring home the prize, we will not rest."

We couldn't find a skate, but everyone in the whole camp was impressed that we found the four-leaf clover. The Gray teamers couldn't! And the mighty Blue Team ended up winning by ten!

Sometime before the night was over, Zoe asked, "Hey, what happened to the four-leaf clover? Do we get it back?"

"Good question. I bet Bick kept it somehow."

"Well, I feel lucky anyhow," she said.

"So do I." And I did. Well, for a while, anyway.

CHAPTER 7

The week went on. Our age group did most activities together, but we got some electives and then we ended up with girls from different age groups.

I had started to get used to Mon Mon. For a day or two, I even lost track of how many days were left. But when I got my first package from home and my mom wrote a mushy note about how much she missed me, I got a little bit homesick. As soon as I read it, I wanted to cry, but I didn't want to do it in front of anyone else, so I held it in. It was weird living in a bunk with absolutely no privacy.

The girls in the bunk all *seemed* nice, but I still wasn't exactly used to how loud Emily was, how neat Claire wanted us to be, or how many inside jokes Nina, Claire, and Emily had. I felt closest to Zoe. Maybe it was because we were both new. Or maybe it was because I felt like I could be myself around her. But it definitely wasn't because of who her dad was.

I wondered whether anyone else recognized Zoe. No one said anything or screamed or screeched or asked for autographs. But maybe no one knew how to bring it up or maybe everyone wanted to give her space. But one thing was sure: I wasn't going to tell anyone.

Anyone at camp, that is. On the night of the scavenger hunt, after I realized who she was, I wrote to Eli and Ari. When I wrote to them, telling them about Zoe, I really didn't know her very well. Even then, I thought for a second before I wrote that I was sharing a bunk with Chase Wagner's daughter. I knew that I wouldn't like it if I were her and a new friend wrote about me that way. But it was way too good to pass up! I told them how weird it must be to have a famous parent and how much I liked Zoe.

I hoped she felt the same way about me.

Zoe and I were taking arts and crafts together. On our third day of class, we left the crafts building and started walking back to main camp. I was pointing out a bird to Zoe, and I slipped on a rock, falling on my arms, all sprawled out. When I picked up my head, I was staring at a snake. A snake!

"MJ!" Zoe shouted.

I screamed. A kind of scare-all-the-birds-from-the-trees type of scream.

Luckily for us, the snake started to go off in the other direction."I can't believe there are snakes! Zoe! There are snakes!"

She laughed and gave me a hand getting up.

"You're laughing? Laughing? There are *snakes,* Zoe!" I shouted.

"You know there are bats too," she said.

Involuntary shiver. "No way. You've *seen* bats? In our bunk?" I was starting to get the creeps.

"Not in our bunk or anything, but flying around at night," she said.

"And that doesn't freak you out?" Bats were definitely on my do-not-need-to-see list.

"I hope this doesn't sound-super-stuck up or pretentious or something, but some summers my family has rented a house in Italy and bats fly around."

I obviously wasn't too surprised that Zoe and her famous family would be off to Italy.

"Bats? *Ew!* What's the point of going someplace beautiful like Italy when you have to deal with creepy bats?" I asked.

"Usually, my mom shoos them off with a tennis racquet," Zoe said.

"Double ew! Your mom must be fearless!"

"Kind of. And kind of not. She'll get rid of bats, for sure. But she wigs out if my sister or I leave the house looking like we 'just rolled out of bed' or something."

"My mom does that too sometimes. Makes me brush my hair or put it in a ponytail."

"My mom hates ponytails. Says they're messy. She's nuts. She's even encouraging me to wear makeup when I go outside of our house! I'm only thirteen! And she wants me to wear designer clothes." Zoe paused. "I mean, I know I'm a little overweight—"

"Oh, Zoe, you are not! Your mom probably has a certain idea about what she wants you to look like. I'm sure it's not about your weight or anything." *It's probably about the photographers who you won't tell me about, because I'm not supposed to know who you are,* I thought.

"What does it matter what I look like? Maybe my mom is trying to make me look prettier because she's embarrassed by me."

"Zoe! How could you say that? You're gorgeous!"

Her suntanned cheeks got redder. "Thanks, MJ. I'm just glad to get away from that—no blow-dryers, no straightening hair, no makeup, no nothing."

"I know. I kind of have the same thing. I mean, not with my mom so much. But at school, you know? Last year everyone started getting way into what they were wearing. Lots of girls started wearing lip gloss and blush. Some even started wearing high heels."

Zoe nodded. "At my school too."

"It's so weird how what you wear or look like can totally kill friendships. This year girls would go to that store Make Up Magic. Do you have that store in London?" I asked.

She nodded.

"Anyway, girls would go to Make Up Magic together and buy stuff. I didn't wanna go. My best friend Ariel didn't really either. But our other best friend, Rebecca, totally went for all the glam stuff. She completely dropped me and Ariel. It was weird."

"Ouch."

"I know, right?" I said. "I definitely don't mind the uniform thing here. We don't even have to think about our clothes." I paused. "I wish we didn't have to worry about makeup either."

"Yeah, me either. I just don't want to think about that stuff this summer. I want to be *freeeeeeee,*" Zoe said.

Maybe it wasn't so great to be Chase Wagner's daughter after all.

That night after lights out, Zoe and I called everyone over to our beds.

"Zoe and I were talking about school and about clothes and makeup and about how we feel pressure to look a certain way," I said. "Have you guys ever felt like that?"

Everyone nodded, and we ended up having a long talk about having to look good. Pressure to be skinny or fit in or whatever you call it.

"Try being African-American and dealing with all of this stuff," Claire said.

"You feel more pressure?" I asked.

"Let's start with hair. Everyone seems to want African-American girls to use hair relaxer and make their hair straight. That stuff is made for animal carcasses, not hair. It burns you. No way I'm doing that. So I keep my hair natural and lemme tell you, people make a fuss. My mom and my friends are all like, 'Why are you wearing your hair like that?'"

"Do you care what they say?" Zoe asked.

"Not really. But, yeah, kind of. It just bugs me. Shouldn't I be able to wear my hair the way I want to?"

"Do you wear makeup?" Nina asked.

"I don't. First off, I hate that they test makeup on animals. And second, I don't want to go there. Or at least I don't want to go there yet. What about you, Neens?"

"You guys know I wear lip gloss. Over the summer I don't wear blush because I get so tan. But yeah, I wear stuff at home. With my skin tone, I look so pale without a little makeup. Rosy cheeks make me feel good."

ZOE

"Then you should have rosy cheeks!" I said. "I think everyone should do what works for them. If makeup is your thing, you should feel good about it."

"Makeup is too fussy for me. I just wanna get up and go," Emily said.

"I wish Astrid was here with her rule board. We could add that for the summer there wouldn't be any judgments," I said.

"Well, I'm down for that," Nina said.

We put our hands together like a sports team. And about fifteen seconds later, Susannah came in and shushed us. Back to life as usual.

CHAPTER 9

The next few days went by in a blur. We had yoga! I taught Zoe the downward-facing dog pose, and we did low cobra together. I did the climbing wall and Emily was my spotter. OMG, she was the best—she totally talked me through it: "Right foot on the pink . . . Go as slow as you need to . . . You got this, MJ!" I made it to the top of the intermediate wall after only having climbed on gym walls at birthday parties!

And waterfront was totally amazing. Once I passed my swim test, thanks to too many swim lessons at the Y, I was allowed to start sailing lessons. Even better, I hadn't had a major attack of homesickness. A few little ones, but nothing that lasted more than rest hour. At least not yet.

But during the afternoon of day six, everything changed. The Sparrows had sorted the day's emails and brought them to our bunk during Shower Hour.

If only Zoe, Claire, or I had been showering when our emails were delivered that day, things might not have gone south.

Wynn from the Sparrows came into our bunk singing, "Mail delivery, mail delivery." She put envelopes on Emily and Nina's beds. She handed me my emails from home and did the same for Claire and Zoe.

Claire did a little email dance. "I got some mail from home! I got some mail from home!"

We were all reading and then after a few minutes, Claire said, "This is so weird. This page in the middle of my email doesn't make sense. It's not for me. And it's got no 'Dear' and no 'from.' It's some middle page."

“Maybe it’s for one of us,” Zoe said. “Read it.”

“Oh, yeah! I see your name, Zoe. It’s probably for you!” Then she sang, “I think it’s for you, I think it’s for you!” Zoe and I laughed.

“Here’s what it says,” Claire started reading. “*We had Chinese food last night at Yang Fan. My fortune said that I will one day prank my sister. Ha, ha. We also went to the beach. As usual, it took forever to get there. Meanwhile, I cannot believe that Zoe Wagner is in your bunk! Wow! That’s crazy! What’s it like to be one step away from a superstar?*”

It took one second for Zoe to look like she wanted to cry. I probably looked exactly the same, because I quickly realized that the email was from my brother. Yang Fan was my family’s all-time favorite Chinese restaurant. Crud.

“I don’t get it. What does it mean that you are one step away from a superstar?” Claire asked.

Zoe looked pale. Her eyes started to well up and she didn't say anything. Claire was completely confused. She dropped the email on her bed and said, "Hey, Zoe, what's wrong?"

I, of course, knew what was wrong. I walked over to Claire's bed where she dropped the email and read the rest of it to myself. The letter was definitely from Eli. At the end of the page he gave me an update on Kreider. So anyone in my bunk could figure out that the letter was meant for me—that is, if they had been paying attention when they asked my pug's name.

I felt awful. Was my entire summer going to be ruined because I did one stupid, insensitive thing? And, I guess, more importantly, did I ruin Zoe's summer? She thought she was flying under the radar.

Sniffling, Zoe managed to squeak out, "It's my dad. He's . . . he's . . . he's—"

"Famous." I completed her sentence.

She and Claire looked at me.

"The email," I said and stopped.

"It was for you?" Zoe said, and then she burst into tears again.

"It's from my brother," I said "I didn't . . . I don't . . . it's no big deal."

"What's no big deal? I'm way confused here," Claire said.

"My dad," Zoe sniffed. "My dad is Chase Wagner."

I could tell that Claire was about to scream; her mouth practically skidded to a stop. Instead she said, "*Hmmm*. I see."

That was it. That was all the help she was going to give me.

"I just . . . I just. I didn't mean anything, Zo." I couldn't figure out what to say. "That day when we did the scavenger hunt, I was looking through my stuff. I have a picture of your dad with his band, and I realized—"

"So you've known the whole time and didn't say anything?" Zoe broke in. She was mad.

"What was I supposed to say?" I cried. "Oh, hey, cool that you're sorta famous?"

"No, you're just supposed to act phony and not stop me when I tell you private stuff about my family. Or you're supposed to let me know that you're just being friends with me because of him!"

"I'm friends with you for you. But you weren't honest either, Zoe. You could've said something." I knew I had messed up, but I wasn't the only one, was I?

"What was *I* gonna say?" Zoe asked.

"Like when you were saying stuff about your mom? She probably wants you to look a certain way because she knows that photographers follow you. But *you* didn't say it."

"That's so unfair! I didn't lie to you," Zoe said.

"Well, I didn't either!" I said.

RULES
Wicked

"I shouldn't be surprised, MJ." Zoe shook her head. "I get this all the time. I just hoped the girls here would like me for me."

"But we do!" Claire said, hugging Zoe. "I didn't know anything. I'm sure that Nina didn't either."

I shot Claire a dirty look. *Thank you very much for throwing me under the bus.* She continued, "I mean, we all love you for you. *Especially* MJ."

Zoe sniffed some more, trying to get a grip. "I'll be okay, Claire."

Claire hugged her again. "We heart you, Zoe."

I definitely got the don't-even-think-about-coming-near-me vibe. There was a wall of ice about ten feet high around Zoe's bed.

"Zoe, I'm so, so sorry that your feelings got hurt," I said.

I was trying to think of some other way to make it better when R^2 banged into the bunk. "Girls, girls, girls!

Tonight we're going to have a picnic and do group-by-group picnic games. Three-legged race. Egg toss. You know, Claire. Tell the girls how fun it's going to be!"

Claire mumbled something, and Rachel started talking about being sure to wear bug repellant.

The thought of having Zoe say she wouldn't want to be on my team made my throat feel swollen—like I was going to cry any minute.

"The games sound like a lot of fun," I said, heading out of the bunk quickly before I broke down. I walk-ran to the tree by our bunk, sat down and started crying. Not loud boo-hoo-hoo crying—just regular sniffles and tears. But, somehow, Nina noticed me on her way back from the shower house and sat down next to me.

"MJ, what's wrong? Are you feeling a little homesick?"

I shook my head. I knew if I started to speak, I would just cry harder.

"What is it? Do you feel okay? Did something happen?"

I stayed quiet, except for some sniffling and Nina said, "I'll just sit here with you, if that's okay."

I nodded. After I calmed down a little, I told Nina the whole story.

"Don't worry, MJ. You didn't do anything wrong. If you knew who she was, it's not a crime to tell your brother. She'll get over it. We just have to let her know that we like her for her."

I nodded. "I definitely do. You know I do."

"C'mon," she said, pulling me up. "We'll go back to the bunk and fix it."

When we walked in and the bells jingled, Zoe looked up at us and then right back down into her lap. Her ice walls were still pretty high.

Nina started to say something when Astrid barged through the door. She was out of breath with excitement. She had no clue that our bunk had just blown up. "Guess what, girls?" she said, breaking some of the tension.

Nina said, "What's going on, Astrid?"

"Lars and I got permission to take you girls into Bridgeton for ice cream after the picnic games!"

Lars was Astrid's best friend from Sweden who had come to camp with her. She was secretly in love with him, but she wouldn't admit it. We had all started teasing her about Lars.

"Are you more excited about getting ice cream or having *Laaaaarrrrsssss* come with us?" Nina asked.

"Very funny. I am wanting to see the ice cream place with all of the toppings. We will go right after the activities. Lars will drive."

Claire said, "*Laaaaarrrrsssss.*" Normally we all would have giggled at that, but only Claire and Nina laughed.

"What about Emily? She's not back from her inter-camp meet," I said.

"She'll be back for dessert. But we have to tell her to save room!"

Once again, Nina said, "*Laaaaarrrrsssss.*" And once again she and Claire giggled, while Zoe and I just stood there. The two of us couldn't deal with our stuff with Astrid in the room. And, really, who knew if we would ever fix things?

Nina whispered to me, "Don't worry. Everything will be okay."

I wasn't so sure and quickly counted backward—42 more days.

At dinner, Zoe sat as far away from me as possible. She kept shooting me looks while I moved the potatoes around on my plate. Worse, dinner was some strange meatloaf thing that had big weird-looking green blobs in it. Wasn't this supposed to be a picnic? Where were the hot dogs and chips?

Once our plates were gone, Astrid walked over and starting singing, "You get some ice cream, you get some ice cream." She smiled and pointed to each one of us. "We'll go into town after the picnic games. I'm so excited to do the three-legged race!"

Claire said, "With *Laaarrrrrrssss*?" But no one laughed or joined in this time.

After dinner, we headed toward the soccer field for our picnic games. Thankfully, when R^2 divided us up, she partnered me with Claire and Zoe with Nina. Emily hadn't gotten back from her swim meet yet.

While Claire and I were tying our ankles together for the three-legged race, she said quietly, "I can't believe that you knew this big thing about Zoe and didn't say anything to any of us,"

Great. I was going to be stuck together with her while she ragged on me.

"I wasn't sure what to do," I said.

"I feel bad that she's so upset," Claire said.

I started to feel my eyeballs swimming in saltwater. I pretended to concentrate on tying our feet together and was able to wipe my eyes with the back of my hand. I didn't want to cry!

"If you had said something to Nina, Emily, and me, we could have figured out how to handle it."

"I didn't think of it. And, anyway, I sometimes don't know how to break into your circle. I mean, you guys have obviously been friends forever. You have all these jokes and camp traditions," I rattled, "and everyone sings and chants here, and . . . I didn't even want to come to this camp."

Before Claire had a chance to reply, Angus called all of the teams to the starting line. The race started, and we took two steps and fell flat. I started to get up, but Claire moved a second later and we both flopped onto the ground.

Zoe and Nina walked over to help us. Nina grabbed me under the arm and pulled me up.

"So, you didn't want to come to camp?" Claire asked.

"Shouldn't we get up and race?" I answered.

"I just wanna know. Have you been miserable this whole time?"

"No. I'm getting more used to it. It's just—" I stopped. "All the singing and you three knowing each other so well. You're all great. But sometimes I felt like I didn't fit in. I've been so glad to have Zoe."

Zoe looked at me.

"*Awww*, MJ. I'm so sorry. I had no idea that you were feeling out of place. Now that I think about it, the first week when we were Hummingbirds *was* really tough. But Em, Neens, and I had each other," Claire said.

I nodded as tears streamed down my face.

Zoe kept her distance, but Nina bent down and patted my shoulder. "You can let it out, MJ. We're here for you," she said.

We were still on the ground, and Emily came banging over. "You guys are dogging the three-legged race? I'll do the wheelbarrow race with one of you." We just looked at her. "*Whaaaaas* up people? Why so quiet?" What's going on? Spill!"

Claire explained what had happened.

Emily nodded, then went into complete bulldozer mode. "Zoe, you know we heart you." Zoe nodded a little. "But you gotta get over it. Everyone here who listens to music knows who you are. You're Chase Wagner's daughter. And no one has wanted to say anything to you. But we all know who you are. And so what? Everyone's probably written home about it. We all know how many brothers and sisters you have, who your first cousin is, and that you've met the Queen."

"She met the Queen? You met the Queen?" Claire blurted.

Everyone laughed. Somehow that broke the ice.

"We all knew. Now you know we know. You have a famous dad. We don't care," Emily said.

Why couldn't I have said that? I would've loved to be able to be that blunt.

"Just to be clear, I didn't know," Nina said.

"I didn't either," Claire said.

Zoe smiled. "I guess because this is a new place for me, I thought I could avoid all of the Chase-mania and be sure that everyone would like me for me, not because they wanted to meet my dad."

"You had to know that we'd figure it out on visiting day, right?" Emily said.

Zoe nodded. "Sure, but you know what I mean."

"Zo, you're my best friend here. I hope you're not still mad. I could tell you the rest of what I wrote to Eli, which was that you were great. From the first day we met, I thought you were amazing."

"You are my best friend here too. I think of you like a sister already, MJ. That's why I got so upset."

"I get it," I told her. "I totally get it."

Then we hugged it out. Maybe there was a random hugger inside of me after all. But I guess this hug wasn't exactly random.

So is it okay to ask about her mom and dad and her life and just be normal? I wondered. I wasn't sure what the rules were, but I wasn't going to ask right now.

Instead I asked, "Is it time to go get ice cream?"

"*Laaaaaaarrrrrrsssss*," was Zoe's reply. And I was pretty sure it was going to be like the song: *Friends, friends, friends, we will always be . . .*

Camp

ABOUT THE AUTHOR

Wendy L. Brandes, an attorney, is quite familiar with the excitement, fun, adventure, trials, and tribulations of summer camp. Initially a reluctant camper, she attended summer camp in the Adirondacks for four years and sent both her son and her daughter to camp in Maine. A published legal writer, Wendy notes that she has had far more fun writing this summer camp series and reliving her days as a camper. She lives in Manhattan with her husband, her children, and her dog, Louie, a black lab.

ABOUT THE ILLUSTRATOR

Eleonora Lorenzet lives and works in Osnago, a small village in northern Italy. After studying foreign languages in high school with the hopes of traveling the world, she attended the School of Comics of Milan. Eleonora has always wanted to be an artist, but if she wasn't an illustrator, she says she'd be a rock star. Or a witch. Or a character from the manga series *Sailor Moon*.

GLOSSARY

batik (buh-TEEK)—fabric design that is created by covering parts of the fabric with wax to keep it from being dyed

burbs (BEHRBS)—short for suburb; a residential district on the outside edge of a city

muffler (MUHF-fler)—part of a car's exhaust system; reduces the noise of a car

carcass (KAR-kuhss)—the body of a dead animal

diversity (di-VUR-suh-tee)—the inclusion of people of more than one national origin, color, religion, learning and other physical or mental disabilities, etc.

electives (i-LEK-tivs)—classes that students can choose to take

initiation (e-nich-e-AY-shuhn)—a ceremony, test, or ritual that someone must complete in order to belong to a group

macramé (mack-kreh-MAY)—the art of knotting cord or string in patterns

narc (NARK)—to tell on someone

paralyzed (pair-a-LIZED)—to be unable to move part or all of the body

set designer (SET di-ZIN-er)—a person that creates the scene on stage at a theater

vice versa (VISE ver-SAH)—with the order reversed; the other way around

GATHER 'ROUND THE CAMPFIRE

1. Why didn't MJ want to go to camp? Use examples from the text to support your answers.

2. Do you think MJ did the right thing when she found out who Zoe's dad was? What else could she have done?

3. MJ and her bunkmates have all felt pressured to look a certain way. Have you ever felt pressured this way?

GRAB A PEN AND PAPER

1. Write a scene from Nina's point of view that takes place after she meets MJ. What does she think of MJ?

2. There are several examples of conflict in this book. Choose one and write about it. What was the conflict? Was it resolved? How?

3. Which bunkmate are you most like: MJ, Zoe, Emily, Nina, or Claire? Use specific examples from the text to explain your answer.

CHECK OUT MORE ADVENTURES!

FOR MORE GREAT BOOKS GO TO

WWW.MYCAPSTONE.COM
WWW.CAPSTONEKIDS.COM